Dolphin Boy

MICHAEL MORPURGO   MICHAEL FOREMAN

Andersen Press

Once upon a time, the little fishing village was a happy place.
Not any more.
Once upon a time, the fishermen of the village used to go out fishing every day.
Not any more.
Once upon a time, there were lots of fish to catch.
Not any more.

Now the boats lay high and dry on the beach, their paint peeling in the sun, their sails rotting in the rain.

Jim's father was the only fisherman who still took his boat out. That was because he loved the *Sally May* like an old friend and just couldn't bear to be parted from her.

Whenever Jim wasn't at school, his father would take him along. Jim loved the *Sally May* as much as his father did in spite of her raggedy old sails. There was nothing he liked better than taking the helm, or hauling in the nets with his father.

One day, on his way home from school, Jim saw his father sitting alone on the quay, staring out at an empty bay. Jim couldn't see the *Sally May* anywhere. "Where's the *Sally May*?" he asked.

"She's up on the beach," said his father, "with all the other boats. I've caught no fish at all for a week, Jim. She needs new sails and I haven't got the money to pay for them. No fish, no money. We can't live without money. I'm sorry, Jim."

That night Jim cried himself to sleep.

After that, Jim always took the beach road to school because he liked to have a look at the *Sally May* before school began.

He was walking along the beach one morning when he saw something lying in the sand amongst the seaweed. It looked like a big log at first, but it wasn't. It was moving. It had a tail and a head. It was a dolphin!

Jim knelt in the sand beside him. The boy and the dolphin looked into each other's eyes. Jim knew then exactly what he had to do.
"Don't worry," he said.
"I'll fetch help. I'll be back soon, I promise."

He ran all the way up the hill
to school as fast as he could go.
Everyone was in the playground.
"You've got to come!" he cried.
"There's a dolphin on the beach!
We've got to get him back in the
water or he'll die."

Down the hill to the beach the
children ran, the teachers as well.
Soon everyone in the village
was there – Jim's father and
his mother, too.

"Fetch the *Sally May*'s sail!" cried Jim's mother. "We'll roll him onto it."

When they had fetched the sail, Jim crouched down beside the dolphin's head, stroking him and comforting him. "Don't worry," he whispered. "We'll soon have you back in the sea."

They spread out the sail and rolled him onto it very gently. Then, when everyone had taken a tight grip of the sail, Jim's father gave the word, "Lift!"

With a hundred hands lifting together, they soon carried the dolphin down to the sea where they laid him in the shallows and let the waves wash over him.

The dolphin squeaked and clicked and slapped the sea with his smiley mouth.
He was swimming now, but he didn't seem to want to leave. He swam around and around.
"Off you go," Jim shouted, wading in and trying to push him out to sea. "Off you go."
And off he went at last.

Everyone was clapping and cheering and waving goodbye. Jim just wanted him to come back again. But he didn't. Along with everyone else, Jim stayed and watched until he couldn't see him anymore.

That day at school Jim could think of nothing but the dolphin. He even thought up a name for him. 'Smiler' seemed to suit him perfectly.

The moment school was over, Jim ran back to the beach hoping and praying Smiler might have come back. But Smiler wasn't there. He was nowhere to be seen.

Filled with sudden sadness he rushed down to the pier. "Come back, Smiler!" he cried. "Please come back. Please!"

At that very moment,
Smiler rose up out of the sea right
in front of him! He turned over
and over in the air before he crashed
down into the water, splashing Jim
from head to toe.

Jim didn't think twice.
He dropped his bag, pulled off
his shoes and dived off the pier.

At once Smiler was there beside him – swimming all around him, leaping over him, diving under him. Suddenly Jim found himself being lifted up from below. He was sitting on Smiler! He was riding him!

Off they sped out to sea, Jim clinging on as best he could. Whenever he fell off – and he often did – Smiler was always there, so that Jim could always get on again. The further they went, the faster they went. And the faster they went, the more Jim liked it.

Around and around the bay Smiler took him, and then back at last to the quay. By this time everyone in the village had seen them and the children were diving off the quay and swimming out to meet them.

All of them wanted to swim with Smiler, to touch him, to stroke him, to play with him. And Smiler was happy to let them. They were having the best time of their lives.

Every day after that, Smiler would be swimming near the quay waiting for Jim, to give him his ride. And every day the children swam with him and played with him, too. They loved his kind eyes and smiling face.

Smiler was everyone's best friend.

Then one day, Smiler wasn't there. They waited for him. They looked for him.
But he never came. The next day he wasn't there either, nor the next, nor the next.

Jim was broken-hearted, and so were all the children. Everyone in the village missed Smiler,
young and old alike, and longed for him to come back. Each day they looked and each day
he wasn't there.

When Jim's birthday came, his mother gave him something she hoped might cheer him up,
a wonderful carving of a dolphin – she'd made it herself out of driftwood.
But not even that seemed to make Jim happy.

Then his father had a bright idea. "Jim," he said, "why don't we all go out in the *Sally May*?
Would you like that?"

"Yes!" Jim cried. "Then we could look for Smiler too."

So they hauled the *Sally May* down to the water and set the sails. Out of the bay they went, out onto the open sea where despite her raggedy old sails the *Sally May* flew along over the waves.

Jim loved the wind in his face, and the salt spray on his lips. There were lots of gulls and gannets, but no sight of Smiler anywhere. He called for him again and again, but he didn't come.

The sun was setting by now, the sea glowing gold around them.
"I think we'd better be getting back," Jim's father told him.
"Not yet," Jim cried. "He's out here somewhere. I know he is."
As the *Sally May* turned for home, Jim called out one last time,
"Come back, Smiler!
Please come back. Please!"

Suddenly the sea began to boil and bubble around the boat, almost as if it was coming alive. And it *was* alive too, alive with dolphins! There seemed to be hundreds of them, leaping out of the sea alongside them, behind them, in front of them.

Then, one of them leapt clear over the *Sally May*, right above Jim's head. It was Smiler! Smiler had come back, and by the look of it he'd brought his whole family with him.

As the *Sally May* sailed into the bay everyone saw her coming, the dolphins dancing all about her in the golden sea. What a sight it was!

Within days the village was full of visitors, all of them there to see the famous dolphins and to see Smiler playing with Jim and the children.

And every morning, the *Sally May* and all the little fishing boats put to sea crammed with visitors, all of them only too happy to pay for their trip of a lifetime. They loved every minute of it, holding onto their hats and laughing with delight as the dolphins frisked and frolicked around them.

Jim had never been so happy in all his life. He had Smiler back, and now his father had all the money he needed to buy new sails for the *Sally May*. And all the other fishermen, too, could mend their sails and paint their boats. Once again, the village was a happy place.

As for the children…

... they could go swimming with the dolphins whenever they wanted to.
They could stroke them, and swim with them and play with them,
and even talk to them. But they all knew that only one dolphin
would ever let anyone sit on him.
That was Smiler.
   And they all knew that there was only one person in the
whole world who Smiler would take for a ride.
And that was Jim.

For Alan, with love from his grandfather – M.M.
For the other Michael – M.F.

This paperback edition first published in 2019 by Andersen Press Ltd.

First published in Great Britain in 2004 by Andersen Press Ltd., 20 Vauxhall Bridge Road, London SW1V 2SA.

Text copyright © 2004 by Michael Morpurgo. Illustrations copyright © 2004 by Michael Foreman.

The rights of Michael Morpurgo and Michael Foreman to be identified as the author and illustrator of this work

have been asserted by them in accordance with the Copyright, Designs and Patents Act, 1988.

All rights reserved. Colour separated in Switzerland by Photolitho AG, Zürich.

Printed and bound in China.

1   3   5   7   9   10   8   6   4   2

British Library Cataloguing in Publication Data available.

ISBN 978 1 78344 750 3